For Arnie, Alice, Hannah, Vanessa and Lavinia

British Library Cataloguing in Publication Data
Tidy, Bill
    The incredible bed.
    I. Title
823′.914 [J]

ISBN 0-86264-268-X

©1990 by Bill Tidy
First published in Great Britain in 1990 by Andersen Press Ltd.,
20 Vauxhall Bridge Road, London SW1. Published in Australia by Century Hutchinson Pty. Ltd., 20 Alfred Street,
Milsons Point, Sydney, NSW 2061. All rights reserved. Colour separated in Switzerland by Photolitho AG, Gossau,
Zürich, Printed in Italy by Grafiche AZ, Verona.
10 9 8 7 6 5 4 3 2 1

BILL TIDY

THE INCREDIBLE BED

Andersen Press · London
Hutchinson · Australia

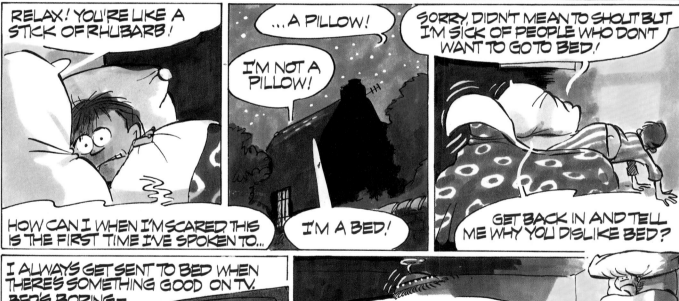

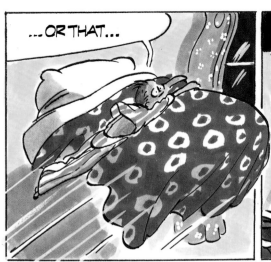

...OR THAT...

OR THIS?

I USED TO BE ONE OF THE 'RED BEDS' DISPLAY TEAM. WE FLEW— OH-OH!

SOMEONE'S COMING!

WHAT A RACKET, TIM. I WON'T TELL YOU AGAIN!

DAD

THE BED WAS TALKING...

..AND IT FLEW UP TO THE CEILING AND DID WHEELIES—

MAKES A CHANGE FROM BEING ATTACKED BY SPACE MONSTERS. GO TO SLEEP OR IT'S THE CHINESE NOSE GRIP. GOODNIGHT!

THAT'S WHAT YOU GET FOR TELLING ON ME!

I WON'T DO IT AGAIN. HONEST!

PROMISE! IF YOU DO I'LL TELL YOU AMAZING THINGS ABOUT BEDS...

..AND WHAT THEY CAN DO!

I PROMISE!

GOOD. KEEP YOUR HEAD ON THE PILLOW SO I DON'T HAVE TO RAISE MY VOICE.

PLEASE, PLEASE, PLEASE, PLEASE—

NOW YOU'RE TELLING ME TO GO TO SLEEP! FIRST IT WAS DAD AND NOW IT'S—

DON'T CRY! PILLOWS HATE SOGGY—

NO! IF THEY FOUND OUT I'D BE GROUNDED. GO TO SLEEP—

OH, SCRODGITTS, WHY DID I MENTION FLYING IN THE FIRST PLACE. I WAS JOKING.

OH I SUPPOSE YOU WERE THE FIRST ONE TO APOLOGISE TO US

MAYBE I COULD TAKE YOU UP FOR THE BIG FLYPAST...

THERE ARE 2 RULES.
1) LIE STILL
2) BE SILENT. OK?

DOESN'T HAPPEN WHEN YOU FLY ME. YOU WANT TO GO?

..BUT YOU MUST DO EXACTLY AS I TELL YOU. UNDERSTAND?

WHAT IF I WANT TO GO TO THE TOILET OR HAVE A BAD DREAM—

YES!

OK. RELAX AND LISTEN... COUGH, COUGH...

WELCOME ABED YOUR BEDDING 777. THIS IS YOUR CAPTAIN SPEAKING. PLEASE CHECK THAT YOUR PYJAMA CORD IS FASTENED, AND YOUR BUTTONS DONE UP. WRIGGLE INTO A COMFY POSITION. TONIGHT IS THE FINAL REHEARSAL...

COMFY POSITION
IN EMERGENCY PUSH KNEES UP UNDER CHIN

..FOR THE GREAT FLYPAST OF THE WORLD'S BEDS, AND WE SHOULD HAVE A SUPERB VIEW OF THE ASTONISHING SPECTACLE AS WE CRUISE AT 50,000 FEET—

50000 FEET!

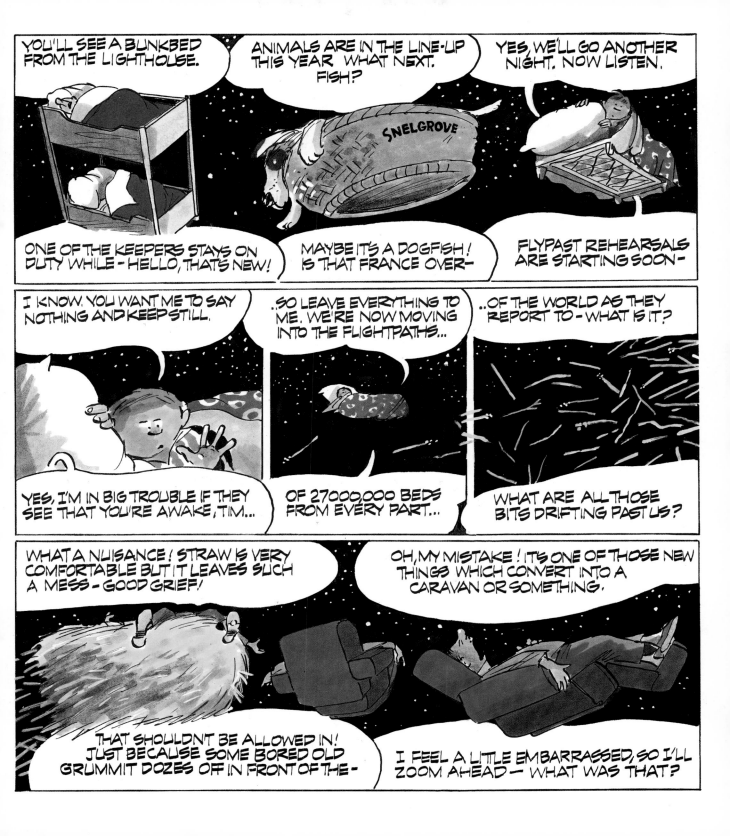

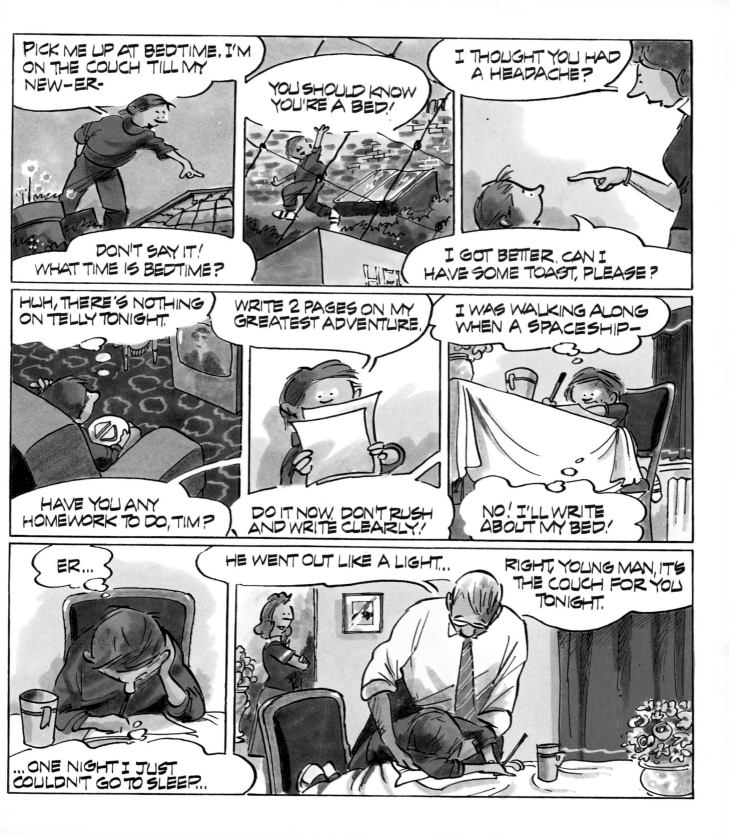

GOODNIGHT, TIM. COME ON, LUV

..MY ADVENTURE STARTED WHEN I PUNCHED MY PILLOW. IT SAID 'OUCH!'

PSST! WAKE UP, TIM.

HUH. IT DIDN'T TAKE YOU VERY LONG TO FORGET ME, DID IT?

SORRY, I WAS ASLEEP - GOSH! YOU LOOK BAD-

SO WOULD YOU IF YOU'D LOST YOUR..

..HEADBOARD AND MATTRESS. JUMP ON!

COME DOWN A BIT!

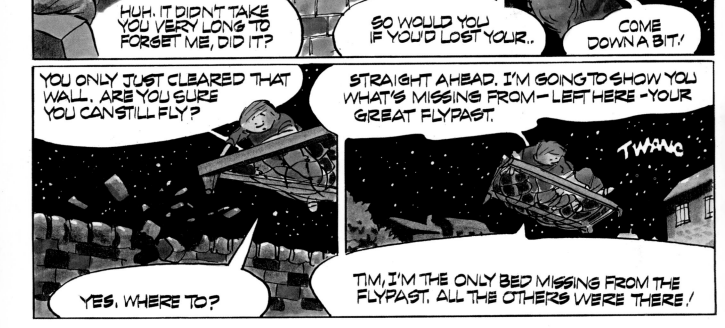

YOU ONLY JUST CLEARED THAT WALL. ARE YOU SURE YOU CAN STILL FLY?

YES, WHERE TO?

STRAIGHT AHEAD. I'M GOING TO SHOW YOU WHAT'S MISSING FROM — LEFT HERE - YOUR GREAT FLYPAST.

TWANG

TIM, I'M THE ONLY BED MISSING FROM THE FLYPAST. ALL THE OTHERS WERE THERE!

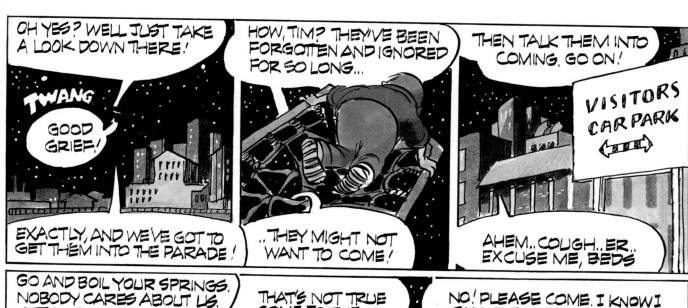

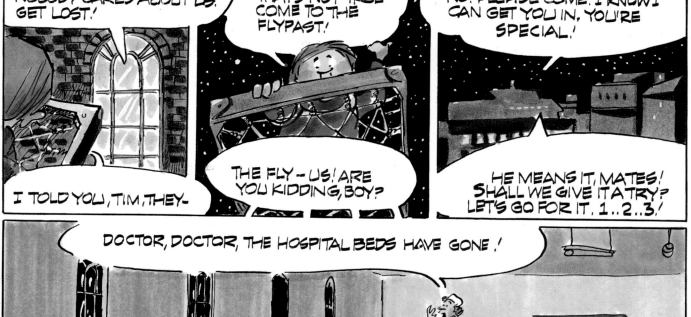

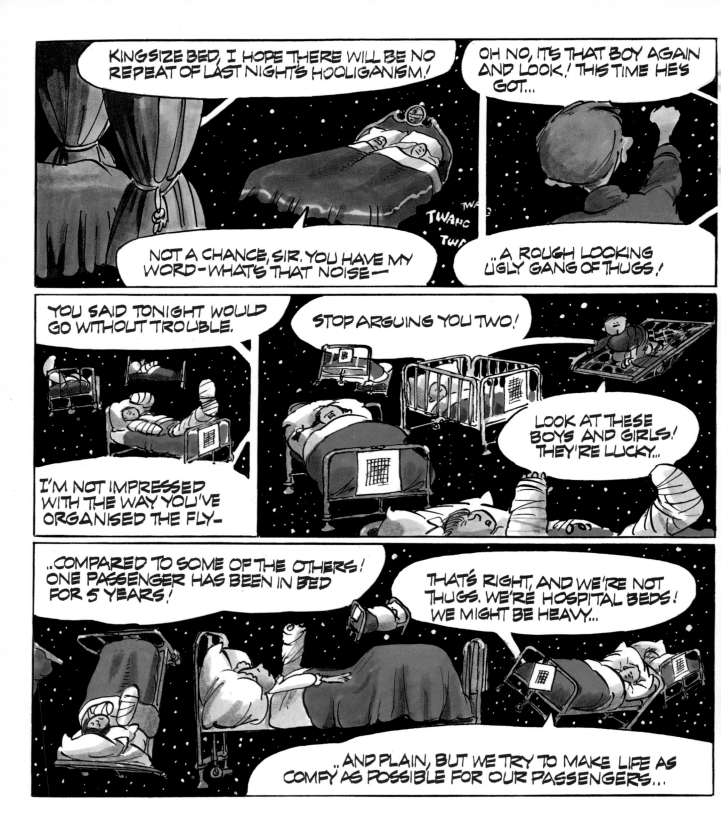

MAGNIFICENT, KINGSIZE. PERFECT FORMATION FLYING WITH THE HOSPITAL BEDS SETTING A FINE EXAMPLE.

VERY IMPRESSIVE, SIR FAULTLESS BEDFLYING!

GOSH, ALL THE BEDS HAVE GONE. HAVE THEY ALL...

..FLOWN HOME WITH THEIR PASSENGERS?

I HOPE SO, TIM. IT GOT A BIT CONFUSING...

.. AT THE END WHEN OLD FOUR POSTER BECAME...

..SO FRIENDLY WITH ALL OF THE HOSPITAL BEDS, BUT I EXPECT...

THEY ALL GOT BACK SAFELY TO THEIR PROPER SLEEPING QUARTERS!

HOW DID THAT GET HERE?

WHEN YOU GO TO BED TONIGHT, JUST BEFORE YOU SLIP OFF TO SLEEP, AT THE VERY LAST MINUTE, SEE IF YOU CAN FLY OFF WITH YOUR BED TO A PLACE YOU'D LIKE TO GO TO AND WHO KNOWS, YOU MIGHT BE BACK IN TIME FOR SCHOOL!